W9-CAE-988

HENRY'S

BY ELLEN LEVINE

FREEDOM

ILLUSTRATED BY KADIR NELSON

BOX

SCHOLASTIC PRESS · NEW YORK

HENRY BROWN wasn't sure how old he was. Henry was a slave. And slaves weren't allowed to know their birthdays.

Henry and his brothers and sisters worked in the big house where the master lived. Henry's master had been good to Henry and his family.

But Henry's mother knew things could change. "Do you see those leaves blowing in the wind? They are torn from the trees like slave children are torn from their families."

One morning the master called for Henry and his mother.
They climbed the wide staircase. The master lay in bed with
only his head above the quilt. He was very ill. He beckoned
them to come closer.

Some slaves were freed by their owners. Henry's heart beat
fast. Maybe the master would set him free.

But the master said, "You are a good worker, Henry. I am giving you to my son. You must obey him and never tell a lie."

Henry nodded, but he didn't say thank you. That would have been a lie.

Later that day Henry watched a bird soar high above
the trees. *Free bird! Happy bird!* Henry thought.

Henry said good-bye to his family. He looked across
the field. The leaves swirled in the wind.

Henry worked in his new master's factory.
He was good at his job.

"Do not tear that tobacco leaf!" the boss
yelled at the new boy. He poked the boy with
a stick.

If you made a mistake, the boss would
beat you.

Henry was lonely. One day he met Nancy, who was shopping for her mistress.

They walked and talked and agreed to meet again. Henry felt like singing. But slaves didn't dare sing in the streets. Instead, he hummed all the way home.

Months later, Henry asked Nancy to be his wife. When both their masters agreed, Henry and Nancy were married. Soon there was a little baby. Then another. And another.

Henry knew they were very lucky. They lived together even though they had different masters.

But Nancy was worried. Her master had lost a great deal of money. "I'm afraid he will sell our children," she said.

Henry sat very still.

Henry worked hard all morning.

He tried to forget what Nancy had said.

His friend James came into the factory. He whispered to Henry, "Your wife and children were just sold at the slave market."

"No!" cried Henry.

Henry couldn't move. He couldn't think. He couldn't work.

"Twist that tobacco!" The boss poked Henry.

Henry twisted tobacco leaves. His heart twisted in his chest.

At lunchtime, Henry rushed to the center of town.

A large group of slaves was tied together. The owner

shouted at them.

Henry looked for his family.

"Father! Father!"

Henry watched his children disappear down the road.

Where was Nancy?

He saw her the same moment she saw him.

When he wiped away his tears, Nancy, too, was gone.

Henry no longer
sang. He couldn't hum.
He went to work,
and at night he ate
supper and went to bed.
Henry tried to think
of happy times. But all
he could see were the
carts carrying away
everyone he loved.
Henry knew he
would never see his
family again.

Many weeks passed. One morning, Henry heard singing. A little bird flew out of a tree into the open sky. And Henry thought about being free.

But how? As he lifted a crate, he knew the answer.

He asked James and Dr. Smith to help him. Dr. Smith was a white man who thought slavery was wrong.

They met early the next day at an empty warehouse.

Henry arrived with a box.

"I will mail myself to a place where there are no slaves!" he said.

James stared at the box, then at Henry. "What if you cough and someone hears you?"

"I will cover my mouth and hope," Henry said.

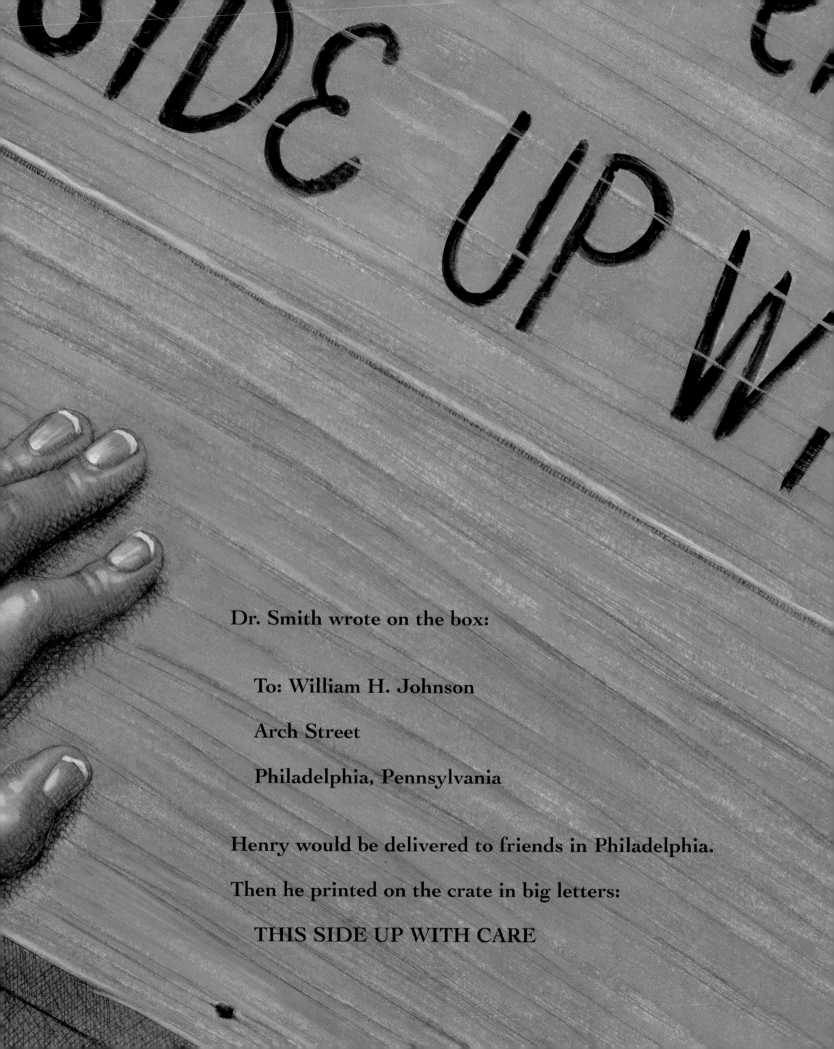

Dr. Smith wrote on the box:

To: William H. Johnson

Arch Street

Philadelphia, Pennsylvania

Henry would be delivered to friends in Philadelphia.

Then he printed on the crate in big letters:

THIS SIDE UP WITH CARE

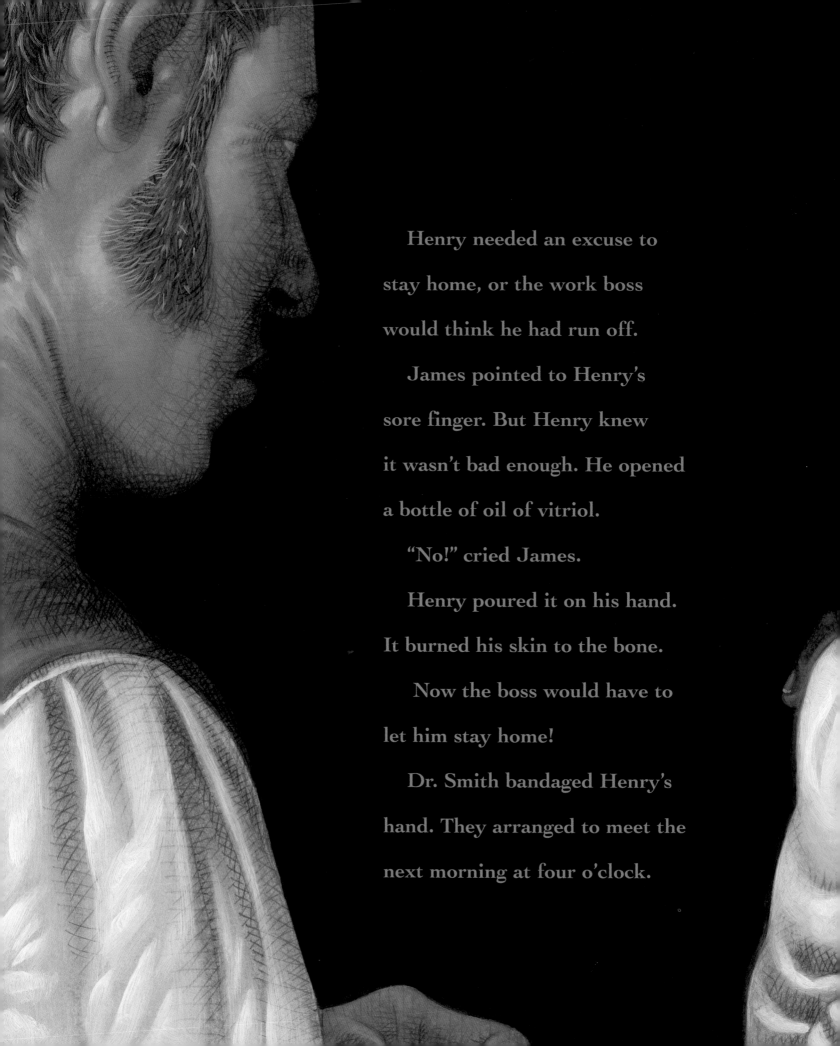

Henry needed an excuse to
stay home, or the work boss
would think he had run off.

James pointed to Henry's
sore finger. But Henry knew
it wasn't bad enough. He opened
a bottle of oil of vitriol.

"No!" cried James.

Henry poured it on his hand.
It burned his skin to the bone.

Now the boss would have to
let him stay home!

Dr. Smith bandaged Henry's
hand. They arranged to meet the
next morning at four o'clock.

The sun was not yet up when Henry climbed

into the box.

"Ready!" he said.

James nailed down the lid.

Dr. Smith and James drove to the station.

The railway clerk tipped the box over and

nailed a paper to the bottom.

Dr. Smith begged the clerks to be careful.

But they didn't listen. They threw the box

into the baggage car.

Philadel|

THIS SI

Hours passed.

Henry was lifted up and thrown again.

Upside down!

He heard waves splashing. This must be the steamboat headed for Washington, D.C.

The ship rode smoothly, but Henry was still upside down.

Blood rushed to his head.

His face got hot.

His eyes ached.

He thought his head would burst.

But he was afraid to move. Someone might hear him.

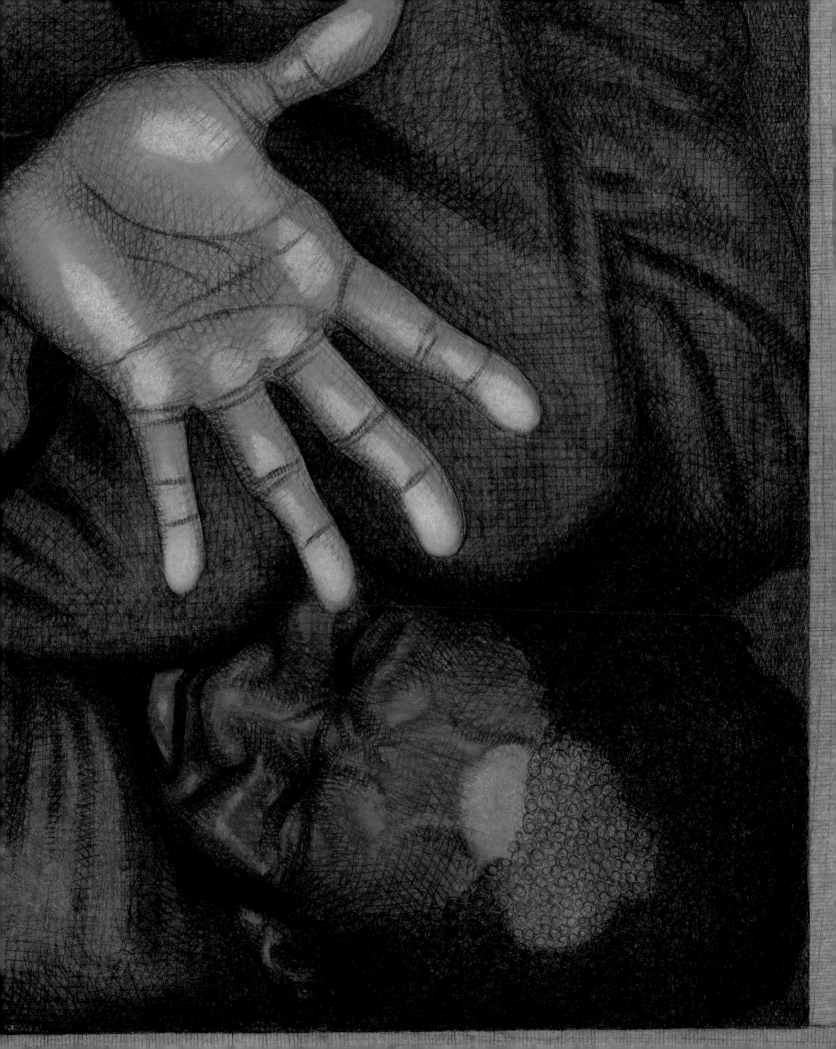

"I'm tired of standing,"

someone said.

"Why don't we move

that box and sit on it?"

said another.

Henry held his breath.

Could they be talking

about *his* box?

Henry was pushed.

The box scraped the deck.

Now he was on his right side!

Now on his left!

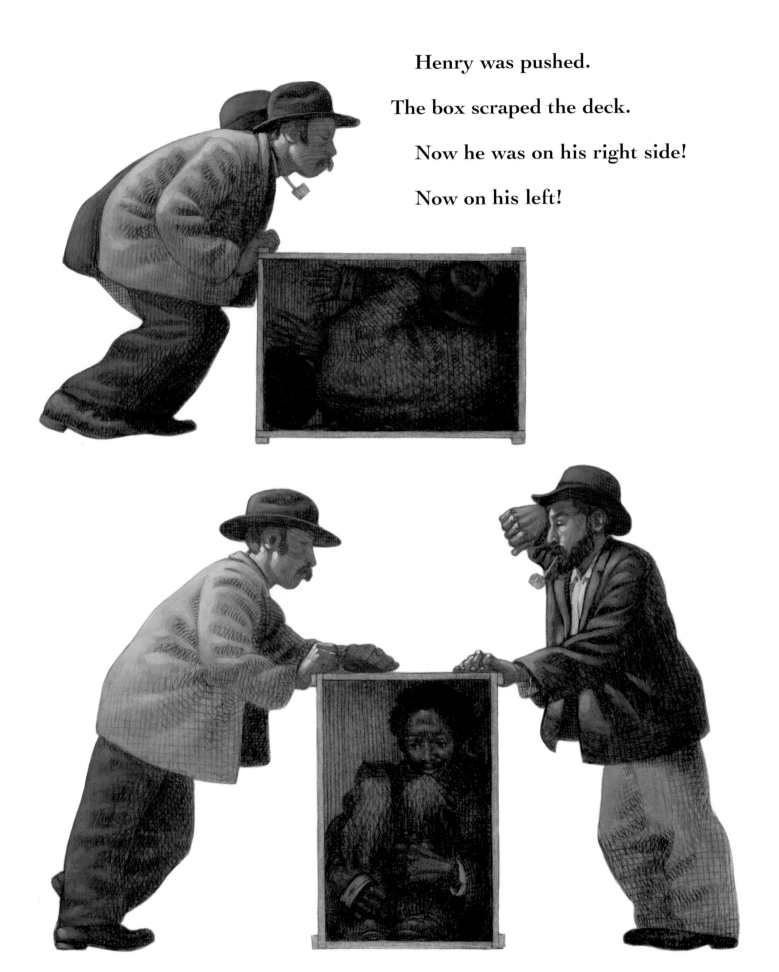

And suddenly, right side up!

"What do you think is in here?" said the first man.

"Mail, I guess," said the other.

I am mail, *thought Henry.*

But not the kind they imagine!

Henry was carried off the steamboat and placed in a railroad car, this time head up. He fell asleep to the rattling song of the train wheels.

He awoke to loud knocking.

"Henry, are you all right in there?"

"All right!" he answered.

The cover was pried open. Henry stretched and stood up.

Four men smiled at him.

"Welcome to Philadelphia!"

At last Henry had a birthday — March 30, 1849, his first day

of freedom! And from that day on, he also had a middle name.

Everyone called him Henry "BOX" Brown.

AUTHOR'S NOTE

IN THE MID-1800s, THERE WERE ABOUT FOUR MILLION SLAVES LIVING IN THE UNITED STATES. Slaves were owned, like tables, or cows, or wagons. Historians believe between 60,000 and 100,000 slaves escaped to freedom. They traveled on what became known as the Underground Railroad.

The Underground Railroad, of course, wasn't a real railroad. It was all the secret ways slaves made their way from the South to the North. The fugitives hid in carts, rode on horseback, walked hundreds of miles through forests and swamps, and crossed flowing rivers in summer and icebound rivers in winter. They traveled any way they could to reach freedom. "Conductors" and "station masters" hid them and helped them throughout their journey.

When Henry Brown climbed into his Freedom Box, he hoped he'd be carried to a safe world. He brought along a small tool to make air holes, a little water, and a few biscuits. His only worry was about being caught. Henry arrived safely in Philadelphia, having traveled 350 miles from Richmond, Virginia, in twenty-seven hours. His story made newspaper headlines in America and Europe, and Henry "Box" Brown became one of the most famous runaway slaves on the Underground Railroad — the man who mailed himself to freedom.

For Mada, who introduced me to William Still

—E. L.

For my mother, Emily Gunter,
for your love, encouragement, guidance, and inspiration

Love, Kadir

BIBLIOGRAPHY

Narrative of the Life of Henry Box Brown, by Henry Box Brown, with an introduction by Richard Newman and foreword by Henry Louis Gates, Jr. New York: Oxford University Press, 2002.

The Underground Railroad, by William Still. Chicago: Johnson Publishing Co., 1970, originally published in 1872.

Text copyright © 2007 by Ellen Levine. Illustrations copyright © 2007 by Kadir Nelson, Inc. All rights reserved. Published by Scholastic Press, an imprint of Scholastic Inc., *Publishers since 1920.* SCHOLASTIC, SCHOLASTIC PRESS, and associated logos are trademarks and/or registered trademarks of Scholastic Inc.

LIBRARY OF CONGRESS CATALOGING-IN-PUBLICATION DATA
Levine, Ellen. Henry's freedom box / by Ellen Levine; illustrated by Kadir Nelson. — 1st ed. p. cm. Summary: A fictionalized account of how in 1849 a Virginia slave, Henry "Box" Brown, escapes to freedom by shipping himself in a wooden crate from Richmond to Philadelphia. ISBN-13:978-0-439-77733-9/ISBN-10:0-439-77733-X 1. Brown, Henry Box, b. 1816—Juvenile fiction. [1. Brown, Henry Box, b. 1816—Fiction. 2. Slavery—Fiction. 3. African Americans—Fiction. 4. Underground Railroad—Fiction.] I. Nelson, Kadir, ill. II. Title. PZ7.L57833Hen 2007 [Fic]—dc22 2006009487

10 9 8 7 6 5 4 3 2 1   07 08 09 10 11   Printed in Singapore   46   First edition, January 2007

Special thanks to Jeffrey Ruggles, a curator at the Virginia Historical Society and the author of *The Unboxing of Henry Brown*, for his careful review of the manuscript. The artwork was created with pencil, watercolor, and oil. The text was set in 16-point B Cochin Bold. The display type was set in Algerian EF. Book design by Marijka Kostiw